Terrible Teacher by Chris Allton

Terrible Teacher
Copyright © Chris Allton, 2019
First published by Chris Allton 2019 via Amazon Kindle Direct Publishing
www.chrisallton.co.uk
ISBN – 9781688719590
Front cover design © 2019 by Chris Allton

For all the teachers and headteachers I have ever had and had the pleasure of working with, all at The Shed for their inspiration and friendship and of course, Layla, my daily inspiration.

Chapter 1

"Layla, are you nearly ready?" Dad shouted up the stairs to me. He was growing impatient, again.

"I'll be two minutes," I answered with little conviction.

"You said that ten minutes ago!"

"I know, I know, I'm coming!" Dad always complained about timing and being late   . He said it was much better to be early and prepared. He continually moaned that I was always fifteen minutes late. Ha, twelve minutes today, I thought to myself.

It was the first day of school. I was now moving into Year Six - Mr Topping's class. The terrible teacher! He was angry and sounds stressed all the time. He is old, not young or cool, but he teaches, year after year, children to be prepared for their tests at the end of the year before they move to high school. He must be good at it to be kept in that class. I think he has been there for ages, like an old teacher, stuck in his ways. Not perfect, but efficient.

He dressed smartly but old fashioned. He wore a brown cord jacket with patches on the elbows. Always a white shirt but with varying ties, often covered in stains (probably coffee or what was consumed at dinner that day). He spent most of his time in class sat at his desk marking books with negative comments, keeping children in for breathing too loud in class, preparing more boring lessons that suck the souls and enjoyment out of children. In fact, other than playground duty or dinnertime duty, he was always in class.

Mr Topping never ventured to the staff room for a drink of coffee - his teaching assistant Mrs Driver always appeared after breaks with a cup of steaming liquid. You know the sort - a metal cup with a lid for "health and safety". His said, "I'm a teacher, what's your superhero power?" I was sure him being a teacher was not a superpower. He was more like a supervillain. I could just imagine him in a secret underground lair, sat behind an enormous modern desk with a giant fish tank behind him taking up the entire wall. No doubt full of piranhas which he could feed naughty children to. He would probably have a chair for visitors to sit in and with the flick of a switch, he could send them disappearing down a black hole to oblivion.

Mrs Driver was his loyal subject - his right-hand woman. She followed his instructions to the letter, whether through loyalty or fear. She seemed very nice, pleasant and, well, normal whenever spoken to in other situations. She ran the school council (which Mr Topping had nothing to do with, thankfully) and she was always nice to me. She must be terrified of him, fearing for her job or the wrath of the terrible teacher when he bellowed in disappointment and disapproval.

Only children in Year Six went into that classroom. No younger children ever entered. Teachers did not send them in, probably in fear of them never returning. Any messages that needed to be passed on were always done by the teacher or teaching assistant but never a child. The children in Year Six always seemed subdued and moved in the corridors in silence and perfectly straight lines. They moved from class to the hall for assembly with military precision, like soldiers on parade. They never spoke: if they did there would be horrific consequences. The headteacher, Mrs Garner, praised them continually for excellent behaviour, yet the children did not do it for her, it was all through fear of him.

I knew some of the children in Year Six. We spoke at playtime or out of school at my swimming club. Strangely, they never had a bad word to say about Mr Topping (don't get me wrong, they did not say anything good either) but I was sure that was through fear.

"What's it really like in there?" I asked my friend Ava, a Year Six victim and fellow swimmer.

"Well, it's very strict. You are not allowed to speak and if you don't complete work you stay in until it is done," came the reply.

"Does he ever smile? Or be nice?" I added.

"You're joking aren't you," Ava laughed in response, "I have never seen him smile once." I gulped and began to panic. This was my life for a year. I thought Mr Fraser was bad (my Year Four teacher), but according to Ava it only gets worse.

Mr Fraser was an angry teacher. He always shouted, and we had to sit in silence all the time.

He was not a particularly great teacher, but he got things done as everyone was so scared of him. You would have thought that he hated children but there was one person he hated more - Mr Topping. There seemed to be a continuous feud between the two whether it be comments on the yard, in an assembly, or full-blown arguments in the corridor. Their classroom doors where nearly opposite each other which caused no end of problems.

I remember on one occasion when I was in Mr Fraser's class, a child from Year Six came in with a note from Mr Topping. Our class was, as usual, in silence, no doubt like Year Six, so the note was passed over without a word. Mr Fraser read the note and immediately, I could see his blood begin to boil. He rubbed his hand through his thinning hair and let out a large cry.

"What?"

The class sat in silence. The angry teacher was poised for action, but who would take the brunt of his fury. "I cannot believe that man. The nerve of him!" He picked up his blue blazer jacket and rapidly dressed, brushing down his pink shirt and paisley tie. He then marched out of the room, showing off his pink socks as his drainpipe trousers climbed halfway up his calves. "Layla, you are in charge."

What this meant was I had to sit there and if any of my classmates, moved or spoke I had to write their name on the whiteboard at the front of the class. This was a terrible position to be put in as I was basically the class grass now. However, there was an unwritten rule in Year Four, whereby if anyone did speak or move it was ignored by the temporary leader and when Mr Fraser returned, the mini teacher informed the angry one that everything had been fine. It worked in everyone's favour, a happy class and not an angry teacher.

As it was my turn to be temporarily in charge, I stood at the front of the class, pen in hand, next to the whiteboard. From this position, I could see the whole class but more importantly, I could see into the corridor. I could see Mr Fraser entering Year Six and waving the note in the direction of Mr Topping. The terrible teacher rose to his feet and escorted the angry teacher into the corridor. I expected a huge argument to follow but instead, a few quiet words were exchanged. Mr Topping remained very calm despite the obvious agitation of Mr Fraser.

Several minutes passed of silent arguing until Mr Fraser screwed up the note and threw it at Mr Topping. He then turned and re-entered the class. As the door opened, we all heard him say,

"I will have my revenge Mr Topping; you mark my words!" Mr Topping stood and gave a menacing glance towards his nemesis and turned and returned to class. "Sit!" came my instructions and I returned to my place silently.

Not another word was mentioned about the incident, until break time when everyone was talking about it on the playground.

"I thought he was going to hit him."

"Did you see how red he went?"

"I can't believe they didn't shout."

"I bet Mr Topping would win in a fight."

The comments continued but no one had an explanation for what was written on the note. Even Adele, who had been the note carrier, had no idea what was written on it.

"Mr Topping was sat at his desk as usual and looked shocked at something he had seen on his computer screen. He then wrote the note and asked me to take it to your class," she explained to the crowd who had gathered around her for more detail.

Further incidents like this continued throughout the year, always ending in squabbles in the corridor. When I left Year Four for Year Five, a relative amount of calm returned, and it was an excellent year as I had Mrs Oliver. She was a young teacher with lots of enthusiasm and her lessons were always fun. She used to make fun of both teachers on either side of her but made us promise not to tell or she would get into trouble. We did everything she said, we trusted her, and she made our days pass with lots of fun educational activities.

I was very sad to leave Mrs Oliver's class. Not only did I learn a lot but the thought of going into Year Six was daunting, not only for me but for the rest of the class. Normally schools have a transition day in July, in preparation for September, but Mr Topping refused. He said he had to keep his children working right till the end of the year, with no expectations.

As the summer holidays passed, I gradually became more and more anxious about going back to school. Dad did not seem too concerned and said working in a class like that would be good for me and get me prepared for high school. In all honesty, I would have rather skipped Year Six and gone straight onto high school. The final night of the holidays had come, and I was in bed, about to turn my light out, ready to go to sleep. Dad came in as he always did, and he could tell something was wrong.

"What's the matter?" he quizzed me.

"Nothing," I lied.

"Tell me please." I took a deep breath.

"I'm scared of Mr Topping." There I'd said it.

"You don't need to worry; Mr Topping will be fine. You will have a great time in Year Six."

"But he's so scary Dad."

"Listen, everything will be ok. Trust me. See how tomorrow goes and we will talk about it again tomorrow. Ok?" I reluctantly agreed, kissed my Dad and turned over to go to sleep. That night I dreamt Mr Topping had a secret torture chamber beneath his classroom where naughty children were sent. I did not sleep much but when I did finally drop off, it felt like I had slept for an hour. Today was going to be tough.

Chapter 2

To truly appreciate how terrible this teacher can be, first, we need to show a scale of almost perfect teachers to terrible teachers.

1. The perfect teacher

2. The laid-back teacher

3. The fun teacher

4. The cool teacher

5. The young teacher

6. The old teacher

7. The stressed teacher

8. The deputy headteacher/ teacher

9. The angry teacher

10. The terrible teacher

Let us see how many of these you can relate to. Teachers you have had in the past.

The Perfect Teacher

The perfect teacher is usually, but not always a female. That statement alone is a little unfair as there are far more female primary school teachers than male. However, overall, perfect ones tend to be female. Their classrooms are perfect - pristine. Everything is laminated and stuck perfectly straight on the wall. There are the exact number of pencils, rulers, etc. required for a table in the pot in the centre.

The reading corner is amazing and looks like a fancy coffee shop, where children would talk in a relaxed atmosphere but they are so inspired to write; the displays are all interactive, showing off the amazing work the children have done; there is a pet in the corner of the room, a rabbit, or something like that, perfectly clean and well behaved; an immaculate teacher's desk, no clutter or junk. This teacher is like a swan. She is calm and collated on the surface, but under the water is paddling at 110mph. She never breaks a sweat, never spills paint, always has a whiteboard pen that works and a class full of children who are always smiling. They have stickers all over the front of their jumpers showing how amazing they have been.

The Laid-Back Teacher

I can guarantee you have a teacher like this and this one will probably be male. He will have his top button open and shirt loose, probably untucked at the back. He has probably got floppy hair that looks a little messy and he is always sat in his chair at the front of the room, no doubt swinging back or even putting his feet on the desk. That is if he could, as there will no doubt be an endless amount of junk on his table that he has not put away: random guided reading books, empty mugs with mouldy coffee at the bottom, worksheet from previous weeks, letters from the office that should have been given out days ago.

Children love being in this class because, if they use their common sense, they can get him to show videos off the internet or watch films. Try talking to a teacher like this about their favourite films and I guarantee they will end up scrapping the maths lesson and letting you watch the film.

The Fun Teacher

This teacher always wears whacky, bright clothes. They will talk to the children at a child's level and do things like magic tricks, join in games on the playground, eat their dinner in the hall with the children or play the ukulele in assembly. This quite often rubs off onto the teaching assistant in the class and they become as equally mad (sorry fun) as the teacher. Their classrooms are chaos because they want every child to have as much fun as possible. It is organised chaos, but still chaos.

The fun teacher appears to not know what they are doing but behind the funny glasses and crazy ties or tights, they know exactly what is going on. They love visiting other classes to share the fun, often to the dismay of the teacher in that room (probably old or stressed teacher).

The Cool Teacher

Lots of teachers try to be like this teacher but a truly cool teacher is a rare thing. They do not have to try to be cool. They are just naturally cool. The way they look, the way they act, the way they speak. Everything they do. When they do assembly, it is an amazing assembly. They probably play in a band or something like that, wear a three-piece suit but without a tie.

Again, the cool teacher is usually a male but not always. They will have perfectly styled hair all the time and even if it does go out of place it still looks great. They do not drink tea or coffee like other teachers: they drink cappuccinos, lattes or double choc mochas. They are seriously cool.

The Young Teacher

Tracksuit, a bottle of water in hand, in charge of PE - these are the traits of a young teacher. They are super healthy and mega keen. That is why they oversee PE: the old, stressed, laid back teachers have not got the time or patience for PE. Leave it to the youngsters they say.

They do club after club, before school, at playtime, at dinnertime and after school. They show off their netball or football skills thinking they are like the cool teacher, but they try too hard. They continually preach about the benefits of exercise, drinking plenty of water and eating salad for dinner (which they never eat as they too busy doing clubs). This teacher will always have a whistle around their neck.

The Old Teacher

This teacher is usually strict and stuck in their ways because they have been for over twenty years. Their favourite phrase is "well it's worked for twenty years so I'm not going to change now". They continually talk about what it was like in "their day" and mention the cane and throwing board dusters at children (even though many children have no idea what a board duster is). They plan very few lessons because they know what they are doing. They leave school five minutes after the children, probably because they need a night of sleep as the day has worn them out. They like quiet so when you are in their class silence is the name of the game.

The Stressed Teacher

The stressed teacher looks like they have the weight of the world on their shoulders. Usually, with grey hair from too much time with children, they worry about everything. What level are the children at? Have I changed their reading books? Are there enough photocopies for the whole class? What happens if the headteacher comes into my lesson?

Never put this teacher in front of a whole school for assembly: they will just crumble. They always seem ill and complain about the amount of work they should do in the staff room, much to the dismay of the rest of the staff. Teachers, children and parents give the stressed teacher a wide berth. They do not know what they may say if they start a conversation with them.

The Deputy Headteacher Teacher

This teacher is the hardest working one in the school. Not only do they have thirty little darlings to look after but they must run the school when the headteacher is busy or away for the day on an important course. They show many traits of the stressed teacher but can hold it together much more. They are always in other teachers' rooms asking for paperwork, explaining the plan of the day or discussing what books are needed for the next staff meeting. They never stop at any point - they do not eat or drink, they never visit the toilet, they are a machine. Children do as they are told, not because they are scared, they just want to let this teacher get on with the million tasks they have planned.

The Angry Teacher

All teachers (except the perfect ones) get angry at times, but this teacher always seems angry. They seem to shout nonstop. They seem to think this is the only way they can control their class. If you are in their class, earplugs are advisable. Like the old teacher, they demand silence in their classroom. No sound is allowed at all. If you were to murmur anything, then the full volume of the teacher would descend upon you (along with spit and blobs of dinner). In fact, it does not matter what you do in their class, you will get shouted at. It is probably better to just accept it and move on.

The Terrible Teacher

The final type is a bit of a mystery, an enigma. Why? No one really knows what it is like in their class until you have been in it. This teacher usually teaches in Year Six and they have traits of many of the other types of teachers with the obvious exceptions: they are not laid back, fun cool or young. They are very secretive, and they hardly ever come out of their room, spending playtimes and dinner times sat at their desks marking huge piles of books. Usually, children are sat in rows, like in Victorian times; the classroom walls are full of information posters about using a protractor or how to use an adverbial phrase. It feels like the heart and soul has been sucked out of the room.

Now you have an idea about the types of teachers you may come across, I am sure it is clear to see that the final one, a terrible teacher, is by far the worst. You will have no doubt met many of these teachers as you have progressed through school or if you are older, you can probably think back to some who were just like that. Either way, the terrible teacher was what I was about to be introduced to. The summer holidays were nearly at an end, I was back at school tomorrow and I was about to enter Year Six with my new terrible teacher.

Chapter 3

Standing on the playground, in my new school uniform, was a little terrifying, to say the least. When you enter Year Six, gone was the pale blue polo shirt and now the white shirt and tie is customary. I say tie, as it was one of those on a piece of elastic around the neck, the kind you can pull up and down when you get a bit bored in class. However, I did not think there would be many children willing to take the risk in Mr Topping's class.

We stood in the yard, huddled in small groups, whispering, worrying, wondering. The minutes were counting down to the bell ringing. Soon the door would open, and that mad, terrible teacher would appear. The thing we had worried about for the six weeks' holiday was about to descend upon us. I complained to Dad before he left for work but to no avail.

"Oh, don't worry, you'll be fine," he tried to convince me. "Last year's Year Six survived, didn't they?"

I suppose he was right. They had all moved onto high school. No one had been brutally attacked or killed by the teacher. How bad could he be?

The bell rang…

The door opened almost simultaneously and there he was. You could tell some of the parents felt the same as the children. A tinge of fear as he marched onto the yard.

"Silence. Straight-line Year Six!" We all jumped to attention. A sergeant-major would have been proud of the line. "In!" And with that, we filed into the cloakroom.

As we walked in, we noted the pegs on the wall had our names next to them. A small symbol was next to each name: a butterfly, a spaceship, a football. No doubt to try and make us feel happy, I thought. Or perhaps the work of Mrs Driver? To try and ease us in. Either way, it seemed to work with some children as they were over the moon with their choice of stickers.

"I have a kayak, he must know I love it and go all the time," Ste beamed with joy.

"Mine's a dog, he must know I want to be a vet," said Laura with delight.

"I love the boat!" added Lorraine. "How did he know I want to join the navy when I grow up?"

This is how it continued, but I was not convinced. Next to my name and peg, there was a picture of a wolf. Why a wolf? I did not like wolves. I could not understand at all why that was there. We had all entered the cloakroom and we heard the door close behind us.

"Go into class and you will see a name tag on each desk. Find yours and sit with your arms folded. Do not make a sound!" We apprehensively entered the classroom. As I looked around, I noticed the display boards backed to perfection but with nothing on them. Nothing to inspire us about our new topics, just blank blocks of colour. The classroom was very tidy, apart from the teacher's desk. There appeared to be many piles of paper and post-it notes spread all over.

I discovered my desk and found I was sat next to Rebecca, my best friend. Looking at my name tag again, I noticed the picture of the wolf. What was that all about? I was incredibly happy to be sat next to Rebecca but very surprised. Why would Mr Topping sit me next to my best friend? Surely this must be some mistake?

Looking around the room, I noticed that many other people were also sat next to their best friends. What was going on? Then I thought I had got it. He was testing us. To see who would talk, show they were happy, be themselves. Then when someone spoke to their friend, he would rip them apart. Treat them terribly. Rebecca and I gave each other a knowing glance, and both knew we were thinking the same. There was no way we were going to get caught out.

Everyone sat in silence, exactly as he had asked. Mr Topping was still in the cloakroom. Mrs Driver was busy ushering children to their seats. Like a conductor waiting for the orchestra to take their positions, he waited. Finally, we were all sat in anticipation of his arrival. He entered the room and calmly closed the door behind him, then walked to the front of the class. We waited with bated breath. What was coming next?

"Good morning Year Six. This is a very important year for you. In several months, you will be doing your tests that will set your grade for your entrance to high school."

Here we go, I thought. Here comes the lecture. Mr Topping, though not overly tall, was still a dominating presence at the front of the class. Even Grace, the tallest girl in the class, who was almost the same height as him, obviously felt intimidated by him. This was unusual for Grace as she always said what she thought.

Last year, we had had guitar lessons on a Friday afternoon. Friday afternoon? Thirty-six children, thirty-four of which did not want to play the guitar, sat for an hour with our guitar teacher pretending to be interested. Grace, however, could not hold back.

"This is so boring. What is the actual point of this?" she would say to Mrs Oliver in Year Five. Today though, there were no comments or complaints from Grace.

Everyone sat in perfect silence, upright like a piano.

"Some of you have spent six years in this school," he continued. "Some of those years you will have enjoyed, no doubt some of them will have been a little tricky to get through, but you are here now in your final year."

I wondered if he was referring to Mr Fraser's class. That certainly was a difficult year, and it was obvious there was no love lost between the two tyrants. As I sat there, my mind drifted back to other classes I had been in.

The perfect teacher had been Mrs Roberts in Reception. Her classroom looked amazing and still does: the younger children love it in there. We had endless fun playing in the sand and water, thinking we were just messing around but learning vital skills to help us develop through life.

My favourite though was the mud kitchen out on the playground. We got to be very messy and we always ended up in a muddy state. I remember daydreaming in Mr Fraser's class, gazing out of the window and wishing I could go back to the days of making cakes from mud and then throwing them at the boys in the class.

Mrs Roberts had a crazy teaching assistant (who fits the fun teacher model) called Miss Dalton. She used to spend her time wandering the corridors. I often wondered if she ever did any work in class at all. She would float from classroom to classroom, causing chaos and distraction in her wake, not once thinking about the mayhem she left behind.

There were however, two classrooms she would never go in. Yes, you have guessed it. Mr Fraser's and Mr Topping's. I do not think even Miss Dalton risked the wrath of those two.

"Layla, are you paying attention?" a voice boomed. I suddenly stopped reminiscing and came back into reality with a bang. "That is not the sort of start I am looking for at all." I was so embarrassed. Everyone was now staring at me. "And you can all stop staring at her, she doesn't have three heads, does she?"

"No Mr Topping," came the reply.

"There is a lot of work to do this year and you will find that if you cooperate with me, you'll find this year very enjoyable."

I felt like saying "Yeah right!" but after being spoken to moments ago I felt it wise to remain silent.

"Now, for our first activity. I would like a diary entry of what you have done over the Summer holidays. First, I want you to discuss it with your partner and then we will look at writing it down in your books."

I turned to Rebecca. This was a good chance for a chat about what we thought about Year Six. We did not need to talk about the things we had done over Summer as most things that had happened, we had done together.

We had been to the trampoline park, walking around reservoirs with our parents, camping at a music festival, afternoon tea, the list was endless. We just had lots of fun doing nothing together.

"So, what do you think of Mr Topping?" I asked Rebecca.

"He's not as bad as I thought," came the reply. Initially, I was a little shocked but as I thought about it, Rebecca was right. He had not been anywhere near as bad as I thought he was going to be. We were all sat in silence, but he had not shouted at us. We had chosen to be silent.

"I'm sure it will be fun when we get used to his rules," Rebecca stated optimistically.

"Hmmm, I guess," I replied, still not completely convinced.

Mr Topping clapped his hands three times.

"One, two, three…"

"Look at me," came our reply as we clapped in response. This was his way of getting the attention of the class and it worked every time.

"Now you have had a discussion, I would like to share with you an example of something I did over the Summer," he continued. With this, he picked up the remote control and turned on the projector so we could all see his piece of writing.

What could a man like this do over the Summer holidays? He would probably sit in his house, alone in the dark, thinking of new ways to upset children and make them cry. He probably spent his days planning boring lessons for us in preparation for our tests. Then at night he probably slept in a coffin or something like that.

What was written on the whiteboard was something completely different.

"Please read it through to yourselves and then we shall read it together," came our instructions. As I started to read, I heard gasps and giggles coming from the other children in the class. "I don't want any talking, we will discuss the text in a second." I read through the text and smiled to myself at the content. This is what it said.

Over the Summer holidays, I worked on many projects: building a shed in my back garden, as I enjoy spending time in my shed away from distraction; tidying away old paperwork, from previous Year Six classes, in my study; walking my dog daily and getting plenty of exercise for myself and, of course, saving the Prime Minister from a deadly attack from a hideous villain.

The terrible crime was instigated by a secret foreign spy, the evil Count Resarf. After years of monitoring this villainous fiend, I could track his whereabouts over Summer to Paris, the meeting place of the heads of state of Europe. Here, I learnt of his dastardly plan to kidnap the Prime Minister and hold him for ransom. Although I was unable to catch the Count, I could save the Prime Minister and receive another medal for my courageous behaviour. Being a teacher and an international spy at the same time is quite challenging, but with the help of my loyal aides, I can continue my secret missions and save the day.

"Right, as you can see, there is a lot of description in this piece of writing. Please pay particular attention to the use of colons and semicolons. Perhaps I could improve my writing by using personification or alliteration. What does anyone else think?"

The rest of the class sat silent. They did not know what to say. I could not hold back.

"Mr Topping, there is a lot of fantasy detail in there, but it isn't very realistic, is it?" There were gasps from around the room.

"Not very realistic? Hmmm. Interesting, very interesting. And what makes you say that Layla?"

"Well, it says that you're an international spy. And… well… you're not are you." I paused. I could not believe I was about to say the next sentence on the first day of a new year to the terrible teacher in the school. "Are you?"

Mr Topping looked up from his desk and grinned.

"What kind of international spy would tell a bunch of kids his secret plans?"

Chapter 4

As you can imagine, no one in the class knew what to say. Was Mr Topping joking? Surely he must be. There is no way he could be an international spy, could there? I have seen James Bond in films and all the cool things he does, but there is not the slightest possibility he could be like that. I could not even imagine him in a tuxedo for starters.

James Bond travels around in fancy cars and has lots of fancy gadgets, whilst always saving the day. He has had a deadly briefcase, x-ray glasses, exploding pens and numerous other devices to help him in his quest.

Mr Topping has a whistle around his neck, attached to his name badge and a special key that allowed him to open external doors at school. This was not the same. No comparison.

The class were quiet, stunned from the teacher's previous comment.

"Shall we continue with the work?" Mr Topping broke the silence. "Who can tell me some ways of improving the text?"

The lesson continued and everyone else in the class seemed to forget or cast aside the comments of our teacher, but I could not. I tried to talk to Rebecca about it as the lesson continued, but she would not join in the conversation for fear of getting into trouble with Mr Topping. So, I was left alone with my thoughts and they were running wild. I had so many questions. Why did Mr Topping say these things? Could it be possibly true? If it was, why is he teaching at my school? The list went on.

Finally, the bell went for playtime. I then realised everyone else was thinking the same as me but were just too scared to say anything.

"He's crazy, isn't he?" whispered Ste.

"He is just testing us," responded Laura.

"Just wait until someone is brave enough to say something about it and he'll jump on them like a ton of bricks," Lorraine added. These were just some of the discussions taking place in the yard as we sat on the big rubber tyres at the edge of the playground.

"I'll say something," I volunteered.

"Don't be daft," replied Rebecca, "You'll get into so much trouble. Please don't say anything – not on the first day!"

I decided to listen to her warning and did not say anything about the subject again. We settled into life in our new class very well and, as it turned out, life in Year Six was not as bad as we first thought it might be. Despite this, Mr Topping was very strict, but he talked a lot about respect and knowing the boundaries of the classroom. We did not understand what he meant by this to start with but the more he spoke about it, the more sense it made. He compared us to a football team: all of us had jobs to do in the room. I do not mean taking the register to the office, giving out books, sharpening pencils or things like that. We did have to do that, but he meant our role in the class. Some of us, he noted, were the comedians of the group. Others were the brains of the class. A few were the organisers and one or two the bosses.

"We are a team. Like a family. We stick together in this class and look out for each other. What happens in this class stays in this class." He made us feel good about ourselves and more importantly, feel safe.

"Remember, if you ever have a problem, or you get into a bit of bother with another child or another teacher, come and see me. No matter how big or small it may seem. Speak to me and I will sort out your issues. Don't retaliate, let me deal with it."

It felt like he was on our side. We still had to work and work hard, but it did not seem to matter because we felt so relaxed. As the weeks passed, we received tremendous praise from other teachers in school. Our class had always been "that class" as we had gone through school. Someone had always got into trouble but done it in a way that had brought the whole class down. Teachers did not want to come into our room. I think some thought we would eat them alive given half the chance.

Now though, we were complimented on our attitude to work, gaining good results in tests we had done at the start of the year. Mrs Garner, the headteacher, commented on how we walked into and behaved during assembly. More importantly of all, it made us feel good about ourselves and we just wanted to continue to impress. Work hard and impress.

We have a behaviour chart in class which is a traffic light system. Everyone starts the day on green and if you misbehave you move down to amber. Do it again and you move down to red. (This is not good). In our time in Year Six, no one moved down the chart. Not because we were scared (though I think initially some of the class dare not breath at times in case it was too loud), but because we enjoyed the positive praise and openness of the teacher if we were good. In fact, most of us moved up on the chart to silver or gold daily. Some children even moved up to platinum, which was a new section only available for Year Six.

"There's one simple rule in this class," Mr Topping had said at the start of the year. "Do as I say when I say it and I will pretty much let you do what you want." This seemed very strange at the start: a teacher telling us we could do whatever we want, but it worked. We just had to follow his rules.

The beauty of it was, that most of his rules were very laid back: we could talk to each other, listen to music, have treats in class if we did as he said. If we did not, these privileges were removed until we had earnt his trust and respect again.

Mr Topping was also not afraid to make a mistake, admit when he had done something wrong or did not know the answer to a question. If someone asked him something and he did not know the answer, they would look it up together. Sometimes I think he just pretended he did not know how to do something or how to spell a word, but the fact he involved us in the process of finding it out made a huge difference.

If he did something wrong on the whiteboard or forgot to give out a newsletter or spelling sheet, he would apologise.

"I'm sorry, it is my fault," he would announce to us. "I will learn from this and not forget next time." He would have quotes on the wall for us to see all the time. Things like…

"Mistakes are the portals of discovery"
(James Joyce)

or…

"A person who never made a mistake never tried anything new." (Albert Einstein)

It took a while for these quotes to sink in for us, but eventually, we got it. We did not have to be right all the time; it was ok to be wrong if we tried and we learnt from our mistakes.

Weeks had passed now and all the children felt much more comfortable in Year Six than they had ever expected. Mr Topping regularly told us that we were the best class in school, we just had to prove it to everyone else. If we stuck with him and trusted him, he would not let us down. We did. And he did not.

One Monday morning, as I was walking around each classroom handing out the registers prior to the bell ringing, I approached Mr Fraser's room. Every day, I had to do this. I knocked on the door with trepidation and waited for a response. I never got one as Mr Fraser was very rarely in his room in a morning but I dare not risk walking into his room and suffering his wrath if I had not knocked.

I knocked. No answer, so in I went. His room had not changed much since I had been in his class in Year Four. The walls were all backed in black backing paper with a selection of coloured borders – nothing fancy – just red, green or blue plain borders. These boards were done to perfection by Mr Fraser's teaching assistant, Miss Noon. She was such an efficient teaching assistant, putting her all into everything she did, but she must have found it difficult with Mr Fraser in charge. She always looked tired and ready for a rest or lie down. Once Kate, a friend of mine, said she had been to the photocopier in the staff room for her teacher and found Miss Noon asleep in the corner of the room. Kate had not even realised she was there. Mr Fraser worked her very hard, giving her long lists of jobs to do, some of the things he should probably be doing himself. She was quite often left in charge of the class or left marking books after school.

The room was sparsely decorated and had little children's work to make you think it was a classroom. It had all the things a classroom should have: a library, computers, interactive whiteboard and a teacher's desk, but it seemed to have no life. Every morning I used to think that was what I expected Year Six to be like.

I walked over to the teacher's desk and placed the register on top, noting as I did, a note with a list on it. It read:

<u>Today</u>

1. Miss Noon to mark Maths books.
2. Get children out of class to avoid distraction.
3. Miss Noon to mark English books.
4. Meeting at 1 pm with Mr Smith (Miss Noon to cover).
5. Order gas canisters.
6. Get revenge on Topping.

These items, other than appearing to give Miss Noon no free time at all, shouted out at me. Especially number 6. I did not know what to think and before I could do anything, the stock room door at the back of the class opened and out walked Mr Fraser.

"You? What are you doing by my desk?" he barked.

"Sorry Sir, just putting the register here, you know, like I do every day."

"Don't get clever with me girl or there will be trouble." Smoke appeared to be coming out of the room at the back from which he had just emerged. Was something on fire I thought? He started towards me, in what I thought was quite an aggressive manner, but as he did the classroom door opened. It was Miss Noon.

"Oh Layla, thank you for the register. Mrs Oliver was just asking about hers. You better get to Class 5 quickly."

"Thank you, Miss," I responded gratefully, "and it looks like your cupboard is on fire, there is smoke coming out of it." We both turned to look and saw Mr Fraser now returning to the cupboard door and slamming it shut.

"Enough child!" he bellowed across the class. "Continue with your errands." I smiled at Miss Noon as I backed out of the room and continued to Class 5 and then my own.

Chapter 5

As I entered my classroom, I found Mr Topping sat at his desk, marking books. He looked up at me as I entered and greeted me.

"Good morning, and how are we today?"

"We is ok," I grinned back. We always greeted each other like this every morning when I dropped off the register.

"Anything to report today from the other classes?" he quizzed. Again, something else he asked every day at this time.

"Well, Mrs Roberts and Miss Dalton were arguing about sand in Reception. They were having a competition to see who could build the best sandcastle. Mrs Entwistle in class 3 was playing on a times tables game on the computer and Miss Howard was stood shaking her head behind her, telling her to get on with some work. And Mr Fraser…" I paused.

"Yes, Mr Fraser?" came the reply. Mr Topping suddenly put down his pen, swivelled round in his chair and gave me his full attention. "Go on."

I stood there, unsure of what to say. He might think that I am a little crazy if I told him what I saw.

"Well… it sounds a bit daft but something strange happened in Class 4." I proceeded to tell him what I had seen: the smoke in the cupboard, the note on the desk and the terrible way he spoke to me.

"I wouldn't worry too much about the way he speaks to you. He's like that with everyone, even the other teachers. But this note intrigues me. Why does he need to order gas canisters? Very interesting."

"What about him wanting to get revenge on you?" I asked.

"Oh, I wouldn't worry about that. That is something that has been going on for ages between us. Nothing new there. And you said he is meeting a Mr Smith at 1 pm today?"

"That's what his note said," I answered.

"Interesting. Very interesting indeed," came the response as he rubbed his chin. "Please keep this information to yourself for now, I need to find out some further information about this Mr Smith." With that, he rose from his chair and left the class, heading down the corridor towards the staff room and offices. I did as he asked and said nothing to anyone, merely sitting in class, waiting for the rest of the children to arrive. As the bell rang, everyone else filed into class and sat down. Suddenly, the door opened and Mrs Garner marched in the way she did.

"Right children, could you please sit down. Mr Topping has an important meeting for a little while so I will take the register and start you off on your Maths lesson today." We all sat down and no one seemed to wonder where Mr Topping was, but I knew it must be something to do with what I had told him. As soon as I had told him he was out of the room and now he has an important meeting? Too much of a coincidence I thought. Mrs Garner completed the register, found out what we wanted for our dinner and then collected in any letters or messages.

"Layla, can you take the register to the office for me?"

"I can but it is normally Ste's job."

"Not today, I have asked you." I stood up and walked to the front of the class. I passed Ste, thinking he would be upset but no, not Ste. He was so laid back he could potentially fall over.

He just shrugged his shoulders as I passed him, giving off an "It's fine, don't worry about it" kind of vibe.

I left the classroom and headed towards the office. I peered into Mr Fraser's room to see if there was any further smoke, but nothing out of the ordinary. Just a lot of children, sat working in silence. No change there then. I knocked on the office door and entered to see the two ladies sat talking at their desk. These were the two Bevs – the secretaries. Bev 1 did not like being called a secretary.

"I am the school administrator," she would say. Bev 2 was sat swinging in her chair, talking to a line of parents at the glass window. She was like the first line of defence, to protect the teachers from angry adults. Today a parent was complaining about children watching films in class instead of doing Maths or English. She wished to speak to Mrs Garner but as she was covering in my class there was little chance.

Next was a lady called Emma who oversaw the PTA (Parent-Teacher Association). She was a little crazy and was currently threatening the office staff with a giant water gun. She was planning on having a giant water fight on the field and thought it a good idea to test it out. The two Bevs did not look impressed and Bev 2 hastily closed the window to avoid a soaking.

I left the office and passed the headteacher's office. As I went by the door swung open and Mr Topping was stood there. He beckoned me in.

"Quick Layla, in here." I expected other people to be in the office if it were a meeting but he was on his own. He was jumping around overly excited about something.

"Is everything ok?" I asked cautiously. "Am I in some sort of trouble?"

"No, not at all. Come and sit down." I sat down on one of the pink office chairs (Mrs Garner's favourite colour) and anxiously waited for Mr Topping to tell me what was going on.

"Right, what I am about to tell you, you may find very shocking and hard to believe but I am trusting you that you will keep it a secret. Can I rely on you Layla?"

"Err, yes," I replied, a little unsure of what was to follow next.

"I'm serious Layla, you have to tell no one about this."

"Ok, I won't tell anyone," I answered, sounding a little more confident this time.

"Excellent. Right, where do I begin? I am a spy."

"I knew it!" I blurted out.

"I suspected you guessed, and after what you told me this morning, I have decided to tell you what is going on." I sat eagerly waiting to hear the next part of the story. I was no longer swinging on the pink office chair but was now sat bolt upright.

"I have been a spy for many years and I am currently working undercover in this school." This confused me. If he was not a real teacher, how did he manage to plan all the lessons and teach so effectively? Surely he did not just make it up as he went along. I quizzed him about this.

"No, I was originally a teacher but through a series of strange events, I was enlisted into the secret service of Her Majesty's government. Since then I have been a teacher and during my non-teaching time and holidays, I am a spy. Mrs Garner knows all about this and is very supportive. She has got my back. There is a devious plan afoot and it is vital that I act soon or there could be dire consequences."

Dire consequences. That seemed a little over the top for our school.

"So, did you save the Prime Minister from a deadly attack from a hideous villain over the summer?"

"I did," came the reply. "The Count is an evil overlord and his plans need foiling all the time. It's a good job I have so many holidays a year."

I laughed at this. I knew teachers had a lot of holidays but I assumed they spent them planning, going on holiday, pottering around in their sheds or going to the pub. I did not expect them to be stopping evil tyrants during their summer break.

"So, who is this Count?" I enquired.

"He is an evil man. His goal is to cause chaos in the world and watch as people panic in his wake. He is a master of disguise and finding him is extremely difficult."

"Have you met him?"

"No never. No one knows his true identity, just the carnage he leaves behind. That is his greatest attribute. No one can catch him as no one knows what he looks like. He has many henchmen who carry out his dastardly deeds. And that leads me to why I am intrigued by your story earlier on. I believe that a certain teacher in this school could be working for the Count and be part of the next evil plan he has concocted."

I gave Mr Topping a knowing smile. I knew exactly who he was on about.

"It would appear that Mr Fraser is ordering gas canisters, with school money might I add, for some plan. My surveillance has led me to believe he is plotting something involving an attack on a public area, potentially involving a high-ranking member of parliament or the royal family. Your information this morning leads to think this may be a gas attack and he is preparing it here in school."

"You've got to be joking!" I gasped.

"I wish I was. Fraser has always been a little bit dodgy and he is not very nice to the kids so this wouldn't surprise me at all. Gas canisters, smoke from his stock room and a mystery meeting today. Something is amiss here and I need to find out what. That is why I need your help."

"Me? What can I do?" I blurted out.

"You are going to be my spy. Fraser won't trust me in the slightest but you. You could be very handy in all this. I have spent the last few months building the trust of my class. That is my job. To make people trust me. I am sorry I haven't been completely honest but I hope you understand why." I nodded, still a little dumbfounded by what I was hearing.

"It is a little too dangerous for you to be involved in this on your own so I think you will need some help. Is there anyone in class you know you can trust? Three or four people who you and I can rely on?"

"I know just the people," I replied. I immediately thought of Rebecca. She could be relied on for anything. She was my best friend and we trusted each other with everything. We spent all our time together and I would find it hard to not tell her any of this. Next, would be Lorraine. She was a little daft at times but could always be relied on. She wanted to be in the navy when she grew up so a secret mission would be perfect for her.

Laura would also be perfect. She was nice and caring. She loved dogs and her kind attitude would keep us safe. Finally, I would have to pick Ste. He was always calm in a crisis with his laid-back attitude. Any problem, whether we could sort it or not, Ste would always make us feel better.

I mentioned these characters to Mr Topping and he agreed.

"That's a good team you've got there. Good loyal friends. Right, let's get down to business."

Chapter 6

"We need to have a special meeting," instructed Mr Topping. He kept looking around as if someone may be watching through the window or peeking through the door. "We will meet in the library at midday. I'll tell everyone it is a booster session so no one will be suspicious."

This was true. Mr Topping was always holding extra booster sessions for the Year Six children in preparation for the tests at the end of the year. The tests were not a good thing but we had to do them and Mr Topping reassured us that if we tried our best, he could ask nothing more of us.

"Right, you better get back to class. I will follow shortly." I left the office and walked back down the corridor to my classroom with a strange feeling as if I was being watched. As I entered the classroom, Mrs Garner acknowledged me with a nod and a wink and I returned to my seat. Rebecca looked at me, bursting to ask questions where I had been, but dare not say anything. A couple of minutes later, Mr Topping opened the door in his usual style. You could always tell when he walked into a room by the sound of the door opening. It was always so sudden. Likewise, you could always tell when Miss Dalton entered a room by the over repetitive knocking, she did on the door.

The morning dragged on so long. Mr Topping was acting as if nothing had happened and I did not get the chance to tell Rebecca what had happened. I managed to whisper that it would all become clear at dinner time but that just added to her confusion and, as we were doing tests all morning, there was no chance to explain further.

Dinner time was approaching. I looked at the clock anxiously. Ten minutes to go. Suddenly, an announcement was made.

"Right Year Six, time for some extra boosting for some of you. Now I know it not the most appealing thing at a dinner time but can I please see Ste, Rebecca, Laura, Lorraine and Layla in the library at twelve o'clock. Rebecca looked horrified, Ste just shrugged his shoulders and Lorraine looked like she was about to sulk on the spot. Laura just smiled and I was unsure what to do so I just sighed and tried to put a sad expression on my face. The kind I did to my dad when I wanted something but he would not let me.

The minutes counted down to twelve and I could see Lorraine and Rebecca getting more and more agitated. Finally, the bell rang and we all stood up and filed out of class.

"Why do we have to do boosting today?" complained Lorraine.

"I have to do dinner duty, I can't waste time doing more Maths work," added Rebecca.

"Don't worry, it'll be fine," Ste responded in his usually laid-back way. "It's only half an hour." I did not know what to say. I knew exactly what was coming and I had dragged my friends into this. I started to feel bad.

"Listen guys, there's something I need to tell you…" They all turned and looked at me. However, before I could say anything, Mr Topping appeared behind us.

"Into the library, quickly now," he ordered. We sat down around the large round table in the middle of the library. The kind that is meant to be used for laptops but is usually over-taken by a teaching assistant who leaves their stuff on it as they work there so often.

"Right, I know Layla hasn't had a chance to tell you as I have purposely kept you busy all morning but you have been chosen for a secret mission."

Lorraine did not look happy whereas Ste just grinned with his arms spread out wide. Mr Topping proceeded to tell the tale he had told me earlier about the Count, about his suspicions of Mr Fraser and his suspicious list and how we had been enlisted as agents for him.

"We will need code names for all of you. Any suggestions?" Mr Topping informed us.

"Code names?" Lorraine complained. Lorraine liked to complain about most things. "Why do we need code names?"

"If I need to contact you without anyone knowing I can use the code name without the worry of compromising any of you," came the response. "I have some ideas. Lorraine, as you want to join the navy when you are older, you shall be known as 'The Captain'. Ste, due to your laid-back attitude you shall be now known as 'Sloth'. Laura, due to your love of dogs, I was thinking of something along those lines."

"No, no," interrupted Ste, "it has to be Popeye."

"Popeye?" quizzed Mr Topping.

"Yes, strong arms, plenty of spinach," answered Ste with a knowing grin.

"Fair enough. Laura, are you happy with this?"

"I suppose so," she replied with a slight smirk on her face.

"Rebecca, your code name will be Tick-tock because of your efficiency with time. Always in the right place at the right time." She seemed very happy with this and clapped her hands together, letting out a little squeal of delight.

"This leaves you Layla. For you, we will have wolf." Wolf again, as was emblazoned on the sticker next to my hook. What was all this about?

"Mr Topping, can I ask, why wolf?"

"You don't know?" he replied with a wry grin spreading across his face.

"I have no idea," I replied.

"Don't you worry, you'll find out soon enough." This left me even more confused. "Anyway, onto more important matters. I have these for you." From his pocket, Mr Topping produced five prefect badges. "I am going to inform the headteacher and the rest of the class that I have made you all prefects. That way we can meet regularly and no one will get suspicious." He sat nodding to himself, proud of his little plan to enable us to get together.

"This is so cool," Ste announced.

"My mum will be so proud," Rebecca added.

"Can I have the blue one?" Laura inquired.

"No, no, no! You're not really going to be prefects. You are my eyes and ears in school. These are no ordinary badges. Look." Mr Topping pushed one in the direction of each of us.

"They're just badges," Lorraine moaned.

"Ah, they may appear to be 'just badges' but they are homing beacons and I can track your position at any time with it."

"Awesome!" beamed Ste.

"It gets better," continued Mr Topping, overjoyed with Ste's enthusiasm. "I can press a button on my phone that will alert you all to danger and I can even communicate with you through them."

"That's just like Star Trek," Ste announced with great delight. He was a bit of a sci-fi geek.

"What's Star Trek?" Lorraine questioned. She was not. Mr Topping and Ste both shook their heads at this proclamation. I grinned to myself as my Gran was a massive Star Trek fan so I knew all about it.

"Wow, you must have loads of cool gadgets, like James Bond," Rebecca added to the discussion.

"You don't know the half of it," Mr Topping replied. "Let me tell you about some of the other things I have, just in case." Mr Topping opened his brown cord jacket and removed from his inside pocket a pen.

"I have one like that in my pencil case," Lorraine announced, quite unimpressed now.

"Not like this," and with a flick of his wrist, Mr Topping spun the pen in his fingers, like an over-enthusiastic drummer with his sticks, and aimed towards the clock. In one smooth sweep, the end of the pen opened and a thin dart fired out and hit the clock face dead centre. "Get the point?" he added. We smiled weakly at his attempt at humour but no laughter came out.

"Your jokes are as bad as my dad's," I responded, giving a true reflection of my feelings.

"Ha, I'll be sure to tell your dad that," he replied. "Ok, what do you see around my neck?" This was a little bit of a silly question. We could see his blue lanyard and ID badge hanging from it. All staff wore one to enable them to get through doors in the school. It looked like a credit card and staff had to swipe the card if they wanted to enter (or get out of) school. On this lanyard was also a whistle which Mr Topping liked to blow – a lot – and a couple of random paper clips.

"There is nothing special about that," Rebecca criticised. "All teachers have one of those."

"Not like this," replied Mr Topping. "It may look like an ordinary lanyard what you can see is a garrotte wire, to attack and disarm any potential foes."

"No way," exclaimed Lorraine. Her interest seemed to be growing now.

"Yes way," replied Mr Topping, "and this ID badge does open the doors at school but it will also open any other electrically sealed door. If a key is required, I can do this." He flipped the card and suddenly a thin projectile emitted from the end – a skeleton key he informed us.

"Next, one of my favourites, the whistle. Blown normally, it is my favourite way of getting everyone's attention. However, if I cover the hole and blow hard, it becomes a sonic whistle and causes those near to lose their bearings and become disorientated."

"Do it now," begged Ste.

"Oh no, I cannot do that," Mr Topping warned, "you'd all be on the floor if I did that."

"Well I'm impressed, when do we get ours?" Ste continued.

"Not a chance," answered Mr Topping. "Well not yet anyway." He then grabbed the paper clips. "And what about these?"

"What about them?" I asked.

"They may look like paper clips, but they are in fact, a strong metal alloy used as carabiners when climbing."

"But if you're climbing, you will need some sort of rope," I quizzed.

"I knew you'd say that, so I give you my climbing rope." With that Mr Topping produced his old-fashioned tie to the fore. "Inside here is a tightly coiled high tension steel wire which will enable me to climb or abseil any face."

We all sat gobsmacked and in slight disbelief until he proceeded to unravel the cable from his tie. Soon there was a mess of wire on the floor in front of him.

"That's going to take some tidying up," Laura joked with a smirk on her face.

"Not a problem," Mr Topping replied and with a twist of the knot at the top of his tie, the wire whizzed back into the tie with ease, diminishing the mess in no time.

"And those are just the things I have on my person. My desk and chair are even more spectacular."

He proceeded to list all the amazing apparatus in his room. He started with his desk, which he informed us had numerous secret compartments to store his secret devices. Some were more obvious and on display. His stapler on his desk stapled paper together, I had seen him do it numerous times, but I was informed that with a twist of the arm, the person stapling would be injected with a high dose of sleeping potion to knock them out instantly.

Next on his desk were his post-it-notes. These again were no ordinary post-it-notes. He informed us that by giving these to other members of staff or children, when they wrote on them, he could get a perfect copy left on the bottom note, without them knowing.

The list continued: an x-ray whiteboard to enable the user to see through items, regardless how thick; nicely smelling stickers that said things like 'Mr Topping says you've done great work', but were actually tracking devices; hand stamps to show children had done good work, but not the one that said 'Terrible work' as this contained a poison; certain rubbers that could be used as a rubber but were actually plastic explosives, set off with drawing-pin detonators; and last but not least on the desk, a hole punch that punched holes in paper.

Mr Topping had always joked about having a cupboard that could be used as a prison cell, but he was telling the truth. If you half pulled out the copy of George's Marvellous Medicine by Roald Dahl to a forty-five-degree angle the cupboard swung forward and the hidden cell appeared.

Then there was his trusty cup – the superhero one. Mr Topping informed us that he had numerous cups made like this and they were in fact grenades. I thought this was a little extreme for a primary school but he told us he always had to be ready. Similarly, a large metal blade in his metre stick seemed over the top but he said it was something that may be needed. This was nothing, however, compared to his chair.

Mr Topping had what looked like a regular office chair with arms. He seemed to spend most of his life sitting in his chair, swinging backwards and forwards, scooting around the room. However, he informed us that by twisting the lever under the chair (that normally raises it up or down) it turned in to a booster chair, with the ability to keep up with a car. As far-fetched as this sounded, we all sat and agreed that that would be something amazing to witness.

Chapter 7

The meeting ended abruptly as we all had to eat our dinner. We had pinned our prefect badges to our jumpers, safe in the knowledge we could all keep in contact now. Mr Topping followed us to the hall where Toni and Ann (the cooks) were arguing about how late we were.

"What time do you call this lad?" Ann questioned Mr Topping.

"Oh, leave him alone you," Toni answered, "he needs feeding up and looking after."

We all laughed at this and the way they treated Mr Topping like he could not look after himself.

"And you lot can stop smirking. Where have you been?" Ann continued.

"They have been with me," Mr Topping interjected. "Prefect meeting."

"Prefects? These lot? You're joking?" Toni grinned.

"I know I was struggling and these were all I could come up with," Mr Topping added. The rest of the dinner hall was relatively quiet with some of the chairs and tables being put away.

"I shall have to eat this quickly," Mr Topping exclaimed. "Fraser has this appointment at 1 pm so I need to be ready for that. I need to check who he is meeting and what the consequences of that may be." He tucked into his jacket potato and salad ravenously. "Fraser and I have history and I for one want to know what he has got planned." He polished off his dinner in record time, handed his plate to Ste (who obligingly took it to the dinner hatch) and bid us farewell.

"When shall we next meet?" I asked.

"Tomorrow morning at playtime. I am on duty so we will have to do it on the playground. I will let you know what is going on with this meeting then too." With that, he disappeared and left the hall. We looked at each other, still a little in shock from all we had learnt today so far.

"Well, I'm going out to play," Ste finally announced to the group, "who's coming?" One by one, we all mumbled in agreement, carried our trays out and left the hall through the door, out onto the playground.

Our playground was just like any other school playground: markings on the floor, tyres to climb over, ropes and balance bars to climb on, and a special area for the Reception children to play in. This was right outside Mr Fraser's windows and he always went mad when the Reception children played out making a noise when his class were trying to work. He would always slam his windows and give Mrs Roberts (and the children) a nasty look.

The children at our school, especially in Year Six, were a little different. We had various groups of people who hung around with each other. There was our little gang (Rebecca, Ste, Laura, Lorraine and I) but other groups existed. We all got on but usually, these groups were all drawn to each other every playtime. There was the cool gang, the boys who thought they were going to be rock stars when they grew up. They had long hair and drew tattoos on their arms in permanent marker so even if they were told to wash it off, they could not. Craig, John and Phil said they were going to form a gang when they grew up if Phil stopped looking in a mirror every time he passed one.

Then there was Victor. Or, as he liked to be known, The Vortex. Victor loved hula hooping. He always had a hoop around his middle and walked around the yard constantly spinning. I am sure The Vortex would even eat his dinner standing up whilst simultaneously hooping if the dinner staff did not tell him off. He was always accompanied by Kirsty who played the music that he could hoop too!

Another pair were Imogen and Anya. These two were the edgy kids: dressed differently, listened to cool retro music, did not care what anyone thought.

Next, there was Mick and Tess. They were always together, holding hands, saying they were in love. Mick always had lots of stories and everyone loved listening to them. He was so good we said he should be an author when he grew up.

Finally, there was Tom, Claudette and Frank. Tom was a piano genius – so good in fact that he played in assemblies. Frank and Claudette were very strange. They called each other Dave. Dave One and Dave Two. Even Mr Topping called them Dave in class which everyone thought was hysterical.

"I wonder who we will have in class this afternoon if Mr Topping is busy," Laura questioned.

Good point," Rebecca added. "I bet it will be Mr Russell." The bell rang at one o'clock as usual and sure enough out walked Mr Russell, everyone's favourite supply teacher. It was always good fun when he was in class as he was an example of a laid-back teacher. This afternoon we were doing art and we could get all the paint out. This did not happen very often so when it did happen, we all made the most of it.

Mr Topping had taught us to be independent and sort out tasks like organising paint ourselves. To Mr Russell, this was a dream as he just sat at the desk and said get on with it.

Rebecca and I were trusted with putting out the paint into the palette trays. Dave and Dave handed out newspaper whilst Victor stood in the corner of the room hooping (he had managed to sneak it in after dinner).

"Put that hoop away Victor," ordered Mr Russell, "I fear we may have some sort of paint disaster on our hands if you continue spinning around there."

We all sat down and started our paintings. Having studied the Victorians in History, we were now recreating paintings of L.S. Lowry and his match stalk men. As we were working hard but chatting quietly, I suddenly heard a beeping noise. The prefect badge Mr Topping had given me was vibrating.

"Mr Russell, can I please go to the toilet?" I asked.

"Yes, but be quick," the response came. I looked at the others in our group as their badges had vibrated also.

"I'll find out what is going on," I whispered as I left the table. Out of the classroom I went and into the toilets, straight into a cubicle. The toilets were not too bad at school. The girls were a lot better than the boys apparently as I had never been in the boys, but Ste said there were always pools of liquid on the floor. I never wanted more details than that, but Ste was always saying he would get a mop to clean the floor. He said he would love to clean to music, but that was Ste!

I closed the toilet seat, sat down and pressed the badge.

"Err, hello?"

"Ahhh, Wolf, is that you?" whispered Mr Topping with a crackle.

"Yes, this is Lay... I mean Wolf."

"Excellent," came the reply, "I have intercepted the subjects and can identify that Mr

Smith is not a pseudonym but is local councilman Mr Smith. Through further investigation and a bit of lip reading, I have managed to find out that Mr Smith is the member of the council who oversees arranging the upcoming visit of the Prime Minister to our town. Fraser is finding out a lot of details of the visit and he seems to be plotting something."

"What do you think that is?" I quizzed, whispering as best as I could in case someone came into the toilet.

"I am not sure yet, but I need you to check something for me."

"Hang on..." I interrupted. The door to the toilets swung open. I panicked. Who could it be? Who has come looking for me? I had not been that long, but maybe Mr Russell had sent someone to look for me, or even worse, he had come himself. I held my breath and stooped down to look under the cubicle door. There before me were a pair of black heels. Though not appropriate footwear, this is what Rebecca wore all the time as she liked to look posh.

"Becca, you scared me! Keep a lookout for me. It's ok, it is only Tick-Tock. You can continue."

"Fraser seemed to be inferring that he was going to do something this afternoon, but I am not sure what his plans are for the rest of the day. I need you to get into the staff room and see what is happening for the rest of the day with him and his class."

"How am I supposed to do that?" I asked exasperated.

"Improvise!" came the response. "Let me know ASAP. Over and out." I opened the cubicle door and saw Rebecca stood in the toilet doorway, looking both ways. "Right, we need to get into the staff room and see what is on the notice board for Mr Fraser's class today."

"How are we supposed to do that?" she repeated.

"That's what I said. Improvise!" We left the toilets and headed down the corridor towards the staff room. As I looked through the thin class window of the staffroom door, I could see Mrs O'Leary doing work at the desk. Mr Topping said that she always sat pretending to work, but really, she just ate sweets on the table and flipped through a file.

"What are you going to do?" asked Rebecca tugging on my sleeve as I was about to knock on the door.

"Make it up as I go along," and with that, I knocked on the door.

"Come in," shouted Mrs O'Leary.

"Hi Miss," I muttered, "we need to get something from the photocopier." I planned to get her to turn around and check and as she did this, Rebecca could look at the notice board. What we did not account for was Miss Prince (another member of staff) sat in the corner of the staff room, cross-legged and eating her late dinner. I panicked and looking at Rebecca I could see she had the same thought herself.

"Ok, help yourself," came the reply.

"Thanks Miss," I replied. I was now completely improvising, stood in front of a photocopier, waiting for a piece of paper to appear that had not been sent. Rebecca was still loitering by the door and more importantly, the notice board. "Nothing has come out yet."

"Really," answered Mrs O'Leary, "are you sure you sent it to print here?"

"Positive," I responded.

"Right, let me have a look," and with that, she got up and started messing with the photocopier.

"Maybe it's out of paper?" Miss Prince added. Within the next minute, Mrs O'Leary had opened every compartment of the photocopier making it almost double in size.

"Maybe your sheet is trapped inside somewhere. Miss Prince, you know about this, don't you?" With this Miss Prince put down her jacket potato and salad and sprang into action. Now was our chance. I looked at Rebecca and nodded towards the notice board. I continued the distraction.

"I think I saw a piece of paper in that section at the bottom."

"Right, let's have a look in there then," Miss Prince decided. Next thing, both members of staff were trying to put their heads as far into the photocopier as they could to find the piece of paper that did not exist. I looked at Rebecca and she gave me the thumbs up.

"I'll go and print another one," I mumbled and started backing out of the staff room. Rebecca had already left.

"Well, we'll fix this for you, don't you worry," came the reply. I nodded politely and smiled and hastily left the staff room.

"Well, what did you find out?" I asked Rebecca with trepidation.

"You are never going to guess where Mr Fraser's class are on their way to now." I thought about it and then it hit me like a lightning bolt.

"Of course, the town hall. I bet that is where Mr Fraser is having his meeting. We need to report this to Mr Topping."

Back in the toilet, I told Mr Topping what we had found out.

"Right girls, you have a new assignment. You need to get into Fraser's classroom and try and find evidence about this gas. Now you'd better get back to class."

We both rushed through the toilet door and straight into Mrs Camps, the Deputy Headteacher and Mrs Pedder, her teaching assistant.

"What are you two up to?" Mrs Camps ordered.

"Err, we have just been to the toilet, Miss."

"For ten minutes?" Mrs Pedder questioned.

"Mr Russell was concerned and couldn't find you." Mrs Camps continued. "He sent for me to come and find you. I think you had better spend some time in the library with Miss Kenyon at afternoon playtime to think about what you have done."

"But Miss..."

"No buts. Do as I say. Now back to class." We returned to the class looking rather sheepish as we did. Mr Russell was not done either.

"You two, get back to work now. I don't want any more time-wasting." We both sat in our places a little subdued. Ste gave us a supportive smile from across the desk and we both weakly smiled back.

"What happened?" he said without a sound leaving his lips. Mr Russell had his eye on both of us so replying was too risky. Then Rebecca did something I had not thought of. On the newspaper underneath her painting, she found a crossword. Very casually, she filled in some of the clues.

3 down – check
4 across – gas
7 across – class
11 down – four

She then hinted with her eyebrows for Ste to come over. As laid back as he could, Ste ambled over to our place around the table. As he approached, he read the crossword clues. A knowing nod followed.

"Stephen, what are you doing?" Mr Russell shouted. You could tell he was getting to the end of his tether with us.

"Just getting some pink paint for my picture." As he did, he purposely knocked over the cup of water for cleaning brushes, all over the crossword. Brilliant thinking, I thought, hiding the evidence.

"Well, I have had enough of this. Layla and Rebecca, I believe you are spending playtime with Miss Kenyon in the library, so Laura and Lorraine, you can tidy up the paint." Laura looked happy at this, Lorraine not so much.

Within the next few minutes, the bell had rung and Laura and Lorraine began cleaning up duty, Rebecca and I headed to the library which left Ste to investigate Year Four.

Chapter 8

As we entered the library, we took a last long look down the corridor as Ste entered Year Four. It was all in his hands now. Miss Kenyon was sat in the library on the computer, as usual. We needed to get out but how?

"So, what have you two been up to?" she asked, concerned why the two of us had to stay in at playtime.

"Oh, nothing Miss," Rebecca answered quickly. "We were just discussing a new way to raise money for school while we were in the toilet. Mr Russell thought we had taken too long so here we are now."

"A new idea eh? Well that sounds interesting," came the reply. I smiled just as Rebecca was but had no idea what she was talking about. We certainly had not been talking about fund-raising ideas, but it dawned on me. Miss Kenyon loved raising money for school. She was always trying some new scheme or project. I suddenly realised Rebecca was working on our escape plan.

"Well," Rebecca continued, "my first idea was to allow children to throw sponges at the teachers every Friday afternoon. They would have to pay, of course, and certain teachers, you could charge more for."

"I don't possibly know who you mean," Miss Kenyon answered with a sly grin. We all knew who exactly would be at the top of the list.

"Layla?" Rebecca startled me. "Don't you have the list of ideas in your tray?"

"Err... yes" I lied. This was a risky plan and I was slightly concerned it would not work.

"Miss? Do you mind if Layla goes and gets the list from her tray? It's full of lots of ideas and I am sure you would find it very interesting," Rebecca continued.

"Oh, what a splendid idea girls," beamed Miss Kenyon, clapping her hands together with excitement. "Just make sure no one sees you; I wouldn't want you getting into more trouble."

"I'll be back as soon as I can," I replied and with that, I was out of the door. Year Six was not my destination, it was Year Four. I rushed into the classroom, avoiding the corridor in case I should be spotted. I burst through the door and closed it behind me.

"Ste? Are you there?" I heard a couple of shuffles and bangs from the cupboard and then a masked figure appeared from the cupboard doorway. Initially, I was unsure who the character could be but due to the laid-back attitude and raised thumbs when the figure saw me, I assumed it was Ste. The mask was removed and sure enough, Ste was grinning underneath.

"This is awesome, a real gas mask!"

"Ste, now is not the time to be saying things are cool. What have you found?"

"Ok, ok, chill," he replied, "I have found a couple of canisters, but also a trolley full of unused canisters and a trolley with no canisters in at all."

"So, what do you think that means?" I quizzed.

"Well, I would say it means there is some gas still here, some has been used already and waiting to be filled and…"

"And what?" I answered uneasily.

"And a trolley is empty which means some gas canisters have been removed, possibly today."

"We need to let Mr Topping know as soon as possible," I ordered. "Good work Ste, I will send the message to him now. Can you write a list of ideas of things to do to raise money for school and take it to the library for Miss Kenyon? Make up some excuse as to why I'm not there."

"Got it," he answered as he disappeared out of the door. I continued to look around by the cupboard and in the trolleys. I picked up one of the canisters and closely inspected it. On the side were a series of letters and numbers.

$C_2HBrClF_3$

I wondered if this was maybe some secret code that only Mr Fraser understood, but then it dawned on me. It must be a chemical formula. I must report this to Mr Topping I thought to myself. I pressed my badge and gave the signal, but there was no reply.

"This is Wolf, Come in please." I began to panic, this was not like Mr Topping, he was always there and he always replied. There must be something wrong. "Mr Topping, please answer me!" Suddenly the bell rang and with a startled jump, I realised I had to get back to the library to explain where I had been to Miss Kenyon and then back to class before Mr Russell got even angrier at me. I hastily left class four and could see Rebecca back on her way down the corridor.

"I don't know what you said to Ste but he is still in there talking about auctioning off his time or setting up an art gallery in the hall. That boy can talk for England."

"We need to get into class but I haven't been able to contact Mr Topping, I think something may be wrong. We need to get to the town hall straight after school."

"Ok," answered Rebecca. This was a plan. We would walk home together normally, past the town hall. The only difference today would be it would be at a much quicker speed. The last forty-five minutes of the day dragged. Sitting looking at the clock seemed to make the second-hand tick even slower. Eventually, I could see the minute hand move round to home time and the bell rang. Rebecca and I were up like a shot and out of the door.

"What's happening guys?" Ste questioned as we were grabbing our bags in the cloakroom.

"We need to get to the town hall, ASAP. Mr Topping is not making contact and we are heading there now. You coming?" I quizzed.

"Of course, count me in." He raised his fist into the air as a sign of group solidarity. He always did this when we were up to something, saying he was proud, or that we were "the man".

"You daaa maaan!" Rebecca and I said in unison. He blushed and followed us out of the cloakroom. We left the school grounds rapidly and met Tommy the lollipop man on the main road.

"What you three up to now?" he asked inquisitively.

"Oh nothing, we're just heading into town, we have some errands to run," Rebecca answered.

"Well you be careful crossing those roads," he warned. He did this every day to every child or adult that came near him. We always thought it was obvious he wanted us to do that as he was wearing a fluorescent yellow jacket and holding a giant lollipop saying, "Stop Children" on it. Still, he kept us safe every day and for that we were grateful. "Oh and tell Mr Topping I'll keep an eye on things here whilst you are gone."

"What?" I replied, shocked at his comment.

"Oh, he's told me all about you guys, He has spies everywhere you know," Tommy replied winking at us with a huge smile on his face. With that, we crossed the road safely and continued down the pavement towards the town hall.

It was not far, a ten-minute walk normally but we flew down the street like a herd of wild horses on the stampede. Past the corner shop where we always stopped for sweets every day, past the barbers where the owner Dave would stand at the window, combing his immense fifties quiff, past the market stalls where I worked on a Saturday with Mike and Sarah making my dad's teas. Then it suddenly dawned on me. Should I let my Dad know where I was?

I panicked for a second but then realised he would not be home from work for a while so I would be safe for a bit. I would just tell him I was with Ste and Rebecca. Technically, I was not lying so he could not go mad at me for that.

As we came to the end of our sprint, up the main street into town, we could see the town hall. It was not a very big town hall. We had been in lots of times with school, into the big room that held civil functions or school concerts.

We had sung in the local schools' music festival earlier this year and spent the whole day there so we knew our way around the building.

Finally, we reached the doorway and entered the town hall. Normally, there would be a doorman of some sort, but not today. In fact, there was no one around at all. We burst through the front entrance and flew up the stairs into the main hall. No one there.

"I bet they are in the council chambers," Ste gasped as he was trying to catch his breath.

"That's back downstairs, isn't it?" I asked.

"Yes, do you not remember from our trip last year when Mrs Driver brought us with the Eco Council. I can't forget when she got cross because some of the class were climbing on the furniture and she said it broke every health and safety law the council had ever set up!" Rebecca answered.

We rushed back down the stairs and followed the signs for the council chamber. Again, there was no one around. It was eerily quiet for a building in the centre of town. Finally, we reached the council chamber doors, two huge, wooden doors with large ornate door knockers on them.

"Do we knock?" Ste asked politely. I ignored this and pushed the heavy doors open. What we saw made us gasp.

As the door opened, it was as if a seal had been broken letting the air out. The kind when you open a bottle of pop.

"Get down on the floor," Ste ordered.

"Why what's wrong?" I asked.

"It's the gas, that's what the noise was as we came in. Here." With that, he pulled his rucksack from his back and pulled out three black objects. "Gas masks. I took them from Fraser's room. Told you I thought they were cool."

Thankfully, we each grabbed a gas mask and fumbled to put them on our heads. They must have been set at adult size but once over our faces, we were able to pull the fasteners and make them fit our heads perfectly. I stood up, a little disorientated, but soon got my bearings. I found it tricky to talk and as I was breathing, I sounded like Darth Vader with a bad cold. Once I had stabled myself, I could see the children from class 4 all collapsed in various positions. Some lying on the floor, some sat in the benches the council members sat in, others in the chairs of the council leaders.

I looked around for Mr Topping and even Mr Fraser but could not see either of them. As I made my way through the array of bodies on the floor, Ste assured me, after his first aid training, that all the children on the floor were unconscious. Behind the main chairs for the council leaders were the private chambers. Rebecca and I headed for the doorway whilst Ste continued to administer first aid. Apprehensively, Rebecca pushed open the door. As it opened, we could see Mr Topping, obviously affected by the gas also, tied to a fancy leather Chesterfield chair. Standing over him was a man wearing a gas mask, a long black cape and a fedora hat.

As we burst in, it surprised the masked gentleman and he rapidly made his exit through a door at the back of the room. Rebecca and I made our way to Mr Topping and with a gentle tap on the side of his face, he awoke with a dazed look over his face.

"Where am I? What's going on?" he asked. I replied but got only one reply. "What are you saying? I can't hear through that mask." I tried again but with no luck so I ripped the mask from my face.

"You're in the council chambers. You have been gassed, I assume, with the gas Mr Fraser had in his cupboard. I haven't seen him yet but there was a strange man in a mask with a hat and cape on."

"That was Fraser. He is the Count. I should have seen it ages ago. It is all so clear now. The only thing I don't understand is why he has gassed a council chamber full of children from his class."

Chapter 9

Mr Topping seemed a little down and despondent following the incident at the town hall.

"I can't believe that Fraser is the Count. I should've seen this years ago," he kept repeating time after time. He seemed dejected.

"Don't worry about it, he's fooled us all hasn't he," Rebecca replied hopefully.

"And as you said, the Count is a master of disguise," added Ste.

"But now he has disappeared , we have no idea of his plan and I've got lots of storybooks to mark after school," grinned Mr Topping. This brought a smile to all our faces. "Come on, let's get you all home."

We walked back to school and went our separate ways, apart from Rebecca and me. She came back to my house and as we walked through the door, we were met by my dad.

"Good day at school?" he questioned before we had closed the door. I did not like to lie to Dad but I felt a little unsure as to exactly what to say.

"Err, well it's been a long-complicated day. Do you want me to tell you about it?" I asked, hopeful the answer would be no.

"Don't you two worry yourselves. As long as you are both happy and safe, that is all that matters to me." He winked, grinned at us and nodded his head in the direction of the stairs. "Go on, upstairs, the pair of you: listen to music, relax, take selfies, whatever it is you guys do."

"Thanks Dad," I replied feeling a little downtrodden but relaxed now I was home. We both went up to my room. I opened the door and was met by the usual mess that is probably expected from a fourteen-year-old girl's room: clothes on the floor, whether clean or dirty; make up palettes and bottles, left open after an early morning rush; half-empty/full glasses, bottles and plastic takeaway cups; a box of half-eaten cereal and an untidy bed, left exactly as it had been exited hours earlier in the day.

"That was a bit strange," Rebecca commented.

"What do you mean?" I quizzed.

"Your Dad, it was like he knew what had happened today." I sat and thought about it for a second and started to agree.

"You think my Dad knows what is going on too?"

"Well you know your Dad; would you be surprised?" I grinned to myself and thought it would not be out of the ordinary for my Dad to be involved in all of this.

Rebecca had now moved on. She had opened the hamster cage and picked up Bubble (the hamster) and was now playing with her on the bed.

The next few hours just dragged by. We did all the usual stuff we do: listening to music, messaging boys, putting makeup on each other and watching silly videos on the internet. Our minds were just elsewhere.

"Poor Mr Topping, I feel so sorry for him," sighed Rebecca.

"I know, he seemed very upset didn't he," I replied. "I wish there was something we could do. We have lost track of Fraser; we don't know his plan and we are stuck here unable to do anything." We both sat there: dejected, forlorn, feeling sorry for ourselves.

93

"Knock knock, can I come in?" It was Dad at the door.

"Yes, come in," I replied.

"Look at you two, lying there feeling sorry for yourselves. How can we sort this?"

"Oh Dad, there is just stuff going on at school and …" I did not know what to say. I could not lie to my dad, but in the same breath I knew what I was about to say would sound crazy. "It's about Mr Topping."

"Ahhh, Toppers. What's he up to now?" Rebecca and I looked at each other with utter disbelief. "Still trying to save the world?"

"You know Mr Topping?" I blurted out.

"Oh yes, we used to play in a band together."

"You are joking!" I gasped. "I cannot believe this. Why didn't you tell me?"

"Well you know I was in a band many years ago. You know I know Mr Topping; I talk to him on parents evening."

"Yes, but I thought that was you just being you, talking to everyone. You know what you're like!" My dad looked at me slightly upset but then a grin came across his face.

"Oh, we played in this amazing rock n roll band called The Wolves. He was such a good singer and charismatic frontman. It's such a shame we had to end but we all grew up and became responsible adults! Well, most of the time."

I could not believe what I was hearing. I could not believe after all this time I still did not know my dad knew Mr Topping.

"So what secret mission is he up to at the moment?" came the next question.

"You know about that too? Is there anything you don't know?" I replied.

"Oh Layla, one day you will realise I know everything. What I don't know isn't worth knowing," came a slightly arrogant reply.

"Ok, ok, I get it, Dad is right as usual. Let me bring you up to date." I proceeded to tell Dad about everything that had happened: becoming Mr Topping's secret agents, the code names, the gas in the cupboard, the visit to the town hall, everything.

"So, what is the plan now?" Dad enquired.

"What do you mean?" I answered.

"Well, what are we going to do now to solve this problem and put a smile on your faces."

"There's nothing we can do, Mr Topping told us to come home."

"I see. Right, I have a plan. Get your shoes on and put that hamster down Rebecca," Dad ordered.

"What plan?" Rebecca asked.

"Well, we need to sort out this mess. Fraser has disappeared without a trace, so we need to find him. We need to find some clues to track his position. So, there is only one place we can go to find that out."

"School!" we both shouted in chorus.

"But look at the time Dad, it is nearly eleven o'clock. I'm surprised you haven't told Rebecca and me to go to sleep yet. I know it's Friday but it's still late."

"Oh, forget that, come on, let's go to school. First, we need some camouflage." Dad then proceeded to root around in my make-up drawer.

"What are you looking for?" Rebecca asked.

"War paint," came the reply.

"You're joking?" Rebecca replied.

"We don't want to be spotted, do we. What have you got?" Dad quizzed.

I rooted around in the drawer and found a black eye shadow.

"I don't know what it is or how it works but I'll give it a go," Dad answered. He then proceeded to smear make up all over his face to make him look like an S.A.S operative.

"Will I do?" he asked as he turned and faced us. We both burst out will laughter at the smeared make up all over his face.

"You look a right idiot Dad," I giggled.

"Well it's your turn next," he responded as he began to chase me around the room with black eye shadow. "Maybe a bit of lipstick too?"

Eventually, we were all ready for action and we set off for school. We did not live far away so walking seemed the obvious option. Rebecca and I walked casually and normally but Dad kept backing up to walls and sliding along; sneaking to a corner and producing a mirror from his pocket to check what was happening; jumping over hedges and crawling under bushes. He was just embarrassing.

As we approached the school, Dad started to pretend he had a walkie-talkie fitted in his sleeve and he kept talking into it saying things like:

"Target in sight, over!"

"We have a bogey approaching!"

"Ten-four rubber ducky!"

Rebecca and I just left him to it but as we moved up the driveway, we saw a light on in school.

"Whose room is that?" Dad asked.

"Mr Fraser's," I replied.

"You don't think he could be in there do you?" Rebecca questioned.

"Well there is only one way to find out," Dad answered. "Let's go and have a look."

As we passed through the school gate, we became a little edgy. As we approached the classroom, we ducked to pass under the window, stopping halfway and sitting with our backs against the wall.

"I'll have a look," Dad announced. He slowly turned himself around and edged up the wall until he could look through the window. Vertical blinds were hanging down and they were closed, but if Dad was very careful, he would be able to look through the tiny gap at the bottom. "There is someone in there, in the cupboard."

"Is it Fraser?" I asked.

"I'm not sure, I can't tell from here. The person just looks like a silhouette."

"We need to go in and take a closer look," Rebecca suggested.

"That sounds like a plan. Let's break in." Dad looked excited at his idea and was off crawling on his knees towards the cloakroom door. Rebecca and I followed, quite unsure as to what may follow next. We found ourselves at the cloakroom door and already my brain was working overtime as to how we would get in. Dad removed what looked like a large pencil case from in his coat and unfolded it on the floor. Inside was a stethoscope and various utensils to try and pick the lock.

"I'm a master at this," Dad pronounced. "Just watch this..." With that, he proceeded to put the stethoscope in his ears and try fiddling with the lock with two pieces of metal.

"Just a thought," Rebecca chirped up, "has he tried the door? Maybe this is the way Fraser got in."

"Good idea. Dad, Dad!" I called in my loudest whisper. No use he could not hear with the stethoscope in. "Dad!" Nothing. I grabbed the round shiny part of the stethoscope and whispered down it. "Dad!" He jumped with surprise and removed the headphones as quick as he could.

"What?"

"Have you tried the door?"

"Well of course…. Err, no I haven't." He looked slightly embarrassed and grinned an awkward smile. Still crouching on the floor, he reached up for the door handle and pulled it down. Click and the door opened. We all looked at each other with a sense of anticipation.

"You two wait here. I'll go in and check what's going on."

"But Dad we want to come too," I complained but he continued.

"Not a chance, you are staying here where it is safe." I laughed to myself at the thought. Here we were about to break into a school at night, inside a criminal mastermind and my dad was in charge. Still, he dared to say he was keeping us safe, but I knew what he meant. "Wish me luck!"

He slowly edged the door open and snaked his way in. The door gently closed after him. Rebecca and I made our way back round to the window to peek in. As we both knelt there, fingers gripping the windowsill, we could see the internal cloakroom door open and the figure of my dad sneak through. No one else could be seen. My dad stood up and looked at us, knowing we would be watching. He looked perplexed and just shrugged his shoulders. He looked around the room but suddenly dropped to the floor.

We looked around and saw the hooded figure backing out of the stockroom pulling a trolley full of gas canisters. He had not seen my dad so far but what would Dad do next.

The answer came very quickly. In an attempt at a heroic move, Dad jumped to his feet and charged towards the shadowy figure. In the process however, he fell over a stray PE bag on the floor and toppled headfirst into a pile of chairs. The stranger turned and looked at Dad but did not react. My dad courageously jumped to his feet and rugby tackled the character to the floor.

Rebecca and I could take no more and stood up, charging round to the cloakroom door. We burst through the cloakroom and into the classroom and could not believe what we saw.

Chapter 10

On the floor, in front of Rebecca and I, was a tangled mess of two bodies. There, before us was my dad and… Mr Topping. Dad had his arm around Mr Topping's neck and, in return, Mr Topping had his legs wrapped around Dad. They were struggling in a stalemate as neither could move. It was obvious neither knew who the other person was.

"I've got him, I've got him," Dad was calling in excitement.

"Will you let go of me you fool," came the reply. The sudden realisation came over Dad's face.

"Toppers? Is that you?"

"Of course it is, now let me go." Dad released his grip and they both collapsed to the floor. "What are you doing here?" Mr Topping quizzed.

"Well, the same thing as you, I guess. Trying to sort this mess with Fraser," Dad replied.

"We came to see if there were any clues in the cupboard," Rebecca added.

"We're just trying to help," I concluded. Mr Topping got to his feet and straightened his clothes.

"Right, well that is what I was in the process of doing before your dad attacked me."

"Sorry Toppers!" Dad grinned awkwardly. "Here to help now." Mr Topping returned to the stock room and exited with some rolled up paper, a gas canister and what looked like a firework.

"Ok, this is what I have got so far." He unrolled the paper and revealed blueprints for a building project. Rebecca and I gazed at it, unsure of what we were looking at. Dad stared intently at it and recognised straight away what he was looking at.

"It's the new cinema in town," he announced, happy with his blueprint reading.

"Exactly, so Fraser must have something planned there. Obvious if you think about it," Mr Topping was looking as equally smug as my dad. I looked at Rebecca and she looked returned the obvious vacant look I was giving her.

"The new cinema in town? When does it open?" asked Mr Topping, returning to teacher mode. I felt like I was in an English lesson answering comprehension questions.

"Tomorrow!" Rebecca blurted out.

"And who is coming to visit to do the official opening?" Mr Topping continued.

"The Prime Minister!" I joined in.

"Exactly, now Fraser has tested the gas and we know it works. So now he needs to disperse it over a wider area. There will be hundreds of people there tomorrow. How could he possibly do that?" he questioned with a knowing grin on his face.

"Gas in the fireworks," Dad butted in. "I bet when they explode the gas will be spread out in the air for all to inhale. Everyone there will be put to sleep and Fraser can kidnap the Prime Minister."

"The fiend!" Rebecca blurted out.

"Good choice of vocabulary," Mr Topping joked.

"Thanks," Rebecca replied sarcastically.

"So, would we be right in assuming that Fraser is probably at the cinema setting up now?" Dad questioned.

"I would think so," Mr Topping replied. "So I had better get there ASAP and stop him."

"But what about us?" I asked.

"What about you?" came the reply. "You have put yourselves in enough danger this evening. Let the professional sort it out. Besides which I have to get there quick and there is only one way."

With that he disappeared out of the room, heading towards his classroom.

"Dad, we have to do something to help."

"I know you want to do something and believe me so do I but Toppers is right. We need to leave this up to him. I think we've all had enough excitement for one evening."

"But Dad..." I argued.

"No buts. Home time."

With that, Mr Topping returned to the class pushing his chair. The trusty chair that he spent many an hour sat in, often with his feet up on the desk.

"Right, time for me to get going. Can one of you get the door for me please?" The three of us looked at each other in amazement.

"Why have you got your chair?" Rebecca asked.

"Chair? This is no ordinary chair. This is the OFFFICExr3i. Allow me to show you."

We had moved through the cloakroom and were now crossing the yard. We passed through the school gates, Mr Topping still pushing the chair. We left the school premises and arrived on the main road into town.

"Ok, you guys get yourselves home and rest. This will all be sorted by morning. I've requested back up so this will all be cleared up by morning." He turned to my dad. "We can go out and celebrate after the official cinema opening when Fraser is behind bars where he belongs."

"Sounds like a plan to me," Dad replied. Rebecca was still looking a little perplexed. She could not quite believe Mr Topping was pushing his chair up the road.

"Why have you brought your chair with you?"

"Patience Rebecca, you are about to see," came the reply. With that, he sat down in the chair. Reaching underneath I thought he was going to lower himself down, the way we all did in ICT sessions in school (continually being told off for it!) but no. He pulled a lever and from the arms of the chair, a control panel revealed itself.

Underneath, a funnel appeared and telescoped from the rear of the chair.

"Watch this," Mr Topping grinned. Then, with the flick of a button, fire shot out of the funnel on the back of the chair, much like an afterburner on a jet fighter.

"See you tomorrow." With the flick of a button, he was gone shooting up the road in his school chair. We watched in amazement as he disappeared around the corner, lighting up the deserted streets with the glow of flames from the back of his vehicle.

"Right, bedtime you two," Dad ordered. Rather subdued, we agreed. We both followed Dad who now looked like a giant panda, due to his smudged war-paint. Rebecca and I tried to discuss what had happened, but we were both too exhausted and fell asleep instantly.

We awoke around midday and both rushed down the stairs to find Dad asleep on the settee. He had been there all night, sat upright with the remote control still in his hand.

"Dad, wake up. Today is the day!" I shouted as I shook him.

"Urghh, what?" he complained. "Morning."

"Technically it is afternoon now," Rebecca corrected him.

"Oh right. Where is my phone?" he asked groggily. He reached into his pocket and pulled out his phone. "Right let's see what today holds. Ahhh, a message off Toppers." It read…

"All well. Fraser apprehended and plan thwarted. See you after the fireworks tonight."

"There you go. I told you there was nothing to worry about. He's got it all under control." Dad seemed quite happy, even though he had nothing to do with the results.

"I guess so," I replied cautiously. Something still did not sit with me quite right, but there was little else I could do about the situation. The rest of the day passed very slowly: Rebecca went home, I arranged to meet the gang later in the evening for the fireworks, Dad arranged to meet his friends also and we went on a joint shopping trip to town for my dad's favourite excursion – makeup shopping.

The official opening of the cinema and the fireworks was at eight o'clock but we decided to meet our respective friends at seven to prepare. As we walked to town, I met up with Rebecca and Ste. We left Dad at a pub with his friend and continued to the new cinema complex. There we found Laura and Lorraine. It was quite a big thing for the town to get the Prime Minister to visit. There were a lot of people gathering already and a stage had been constructed with different bands and dance troupes performing.

"Let's get to the front," Laura said. "Some guy is playing Irish songs and you know how much I love that." Lorraine shook her head in disbelief, Ste just shrugged his shoulders and we all followed to the barriers at the front of the stage.

More and more people moved into the pedestrian area in front of the cinema awaiting the fireworks and the arrival of the Prime Minister. Beyond the stage stood the looming complex of the cinema, shops and bowling alley and perched on top I could see the silhouette of fireworks before launch.

Thank goodness Mr Topping sorted this out, I thought to myself. No more would I see the black cape and fedora of Count Resarf. The giant digital clock above the stage was counting down to eight o'clock showing twenty minutes left. Laura was beside herself with excitement about the music being played. Lorraine had gone off to find one of her other friends which left Ste, Rebecca and me.

"I'm still a bit worried," Ste mumbled. Rebecca and I looked at each other in amazement. Ste was the most laid-back person in the world. For him to worry about something must make it very serious.

"What is it?" I asked.

"It's just something about that message you told me Mr Topping sent your dad. It doesn't sound like the sort of thing he would say. More like something Mr Fraser would say. It was far too formal for Mr Topping," explained Ste. "I've even brought a gas mask just in case." He opened his rucksack and sure enough, there was the gas mask we had used at the town hall.

"So, what are you thinking?" Rebecca asked.

"Let's go and have a look around, it won't hurt will it," he went on.

"Ok, that sounds like a plan," I agreed. We looked at the clock and it was getting closer to eight. We could not get in through the main doors of the cinema as it was not officially open, so we circled the building to look for a different entrance. We came across a service at the door at the rear with a man all dressed in fluorescent clothes. He looked like he never took them off as they appeared a bit grubby. They were still doing some final work inside the building, leaving it to the last minute.

"I've got this," Rebecca announced. "Be ready to sneak in". In her usual confident self, she walked up to the man at the door. "Excuse me, is there a health and safety representative around here. I have fallen on a loose paving stone and hurt my ankle.

"Err... I'm not sure, you'll need to speak to the boss." He looked a little uneasy being bossed around by a child but Rebecca certainly had his attention. She had positioned herself facing us so the man had his back to us, next to the open door.

Suddenly she collapsed to the floor, clutching her ankle, complaining about suing the council for negligence. Now was our chance.

"Come on," ordered Ste and he dashed for the door. I followed obediently and we made it into the new cinema complex. It smelt very new and clean inside, almost like a new car smell.

"We need to get to the roof and check the fireworks," I suggested.

"Good idea," Ste agreed. We found a staircase suitable for fire escapes and started the long climb up eight flights of stairs. Eventually, we reached the roof and carefully opened the fire door at the top. The sound of the crowd far below greeted us and we could hear cheers.

"That'll be the Prime Minister I bet," I guessed. We edged out onto the roof and were shocked at what we saw. There, in between various firework stations and pyrotechnics, was Mr Topping, tied to a giant Catherine Wheel, the kind that, when lit, spun violently emitting lots of sparks and flames.

"You know what this means don't you?" I asked Ste.

"Fraser is still here?"

"Yes, this was all a trap. The plan is still on." I checked my watch and saw there were minutes before the eight o'clock deadline. If we did not rescue Mr Topping before eight, he would literally be part of the display and go up in flames.

"You rescue Mr Topping and I'll try to deactivate the fireworks," Ste ordered. I nodded and set off across the roof. I approached the captive and saw that he was unconscious. I tried shaking his leg in an attempt to revive him, but nothing. I turned to look at the control panel, expecting to see Ste dismantling it, but no. There was the figure in a black cape, gas mask and fedora – Count Resarf.

"Too late child, you have failed again, and it's not even eight o'clock." With that, he started to press buttons on the podium in front of him. One of the stations exploded into life, firing rockets far into the darkening sky.

"Wake up Mr Topping," I cried. Another volley of fireworks went up into the sky to the "ooh's" and "ahh's" of the crowd below. They did not even seem to care it had not reached eight o'clock. There seemed to be no stopping the Count now and as the noise of the fireworks died the gas began to fell. I found my throat tightening and struggle to gasp for air. The entire rooftop was filled with smoke and I could not see where the Count was now. All I knew I had to get Mr Topping off the Catherine wheel before the button was pressed. I gave one last attempt to shake Mr Topping awake but I was struggling to breathe and see anything now.

Suddenly I felt a hand grabbing my leg. My time had run out. The Count had come for me. I turned to try and shake the grasp off my leg but it was not the Count. It was Ste, in his gas mask. He pulled me down to his level. Suddenly he ripped the mask off his face and spoke to me.

"You must save Mr Topping; you can do this. You da man!" I placed the gas mask over my face and watch as my friend collapsed in a heap on the floor.

"Ste!" but there was nothing, he was fast asleep on the floor. Now I could breathe, I got to my feet and started to untie Mr Topping. There was no point in trying to wake him, he would be gassed by now if I had woken him.

Eventually, I got his binds free and he fell to the floor. Now for the Count. The smoke was very thick upon the roof. It was very quiet below and I assumed the crowd was now sleeping. Wearing an oversized gas mask did not help either. I stumbled around in the fog and assumed the Count was doing the same. Sure enough, our paths crossed, and we bumped into each other but then disappeared in the fog. This slightly surreal game of Blind Man's Bluff led to a comedy scene of two people trying to stop each other on a smoke-filled rooftop.

As we moved from station to station, occasionally bumping into each other, the smoke began to clear. I saw the Count stumbling, arms spread in front of him, heading towards the Catherine wheel. Now was my chance. I headed towards the control station and waited for my moment. It did not take long. The Count in all his planning and preparation did not expect to have sleeping bodies on the rooftop. As he blindly headed towards the Catherine Wheel, he did not see the sleeping Ste on the floor and with a stumble, he tripped over Ste and went headfirst into the Catherine wheel.

Now was my chance, but which button to press. Bearing in mind the audience was already asleep for the previous explosions I decided to press everything. With a sudden burst of sparks, the Catherine wheel burst into life and there, like a human hamster, the Count spun round and round and round.

Eventually, the fireworks, explosions and smoke cleared. The Count was a tangled mess of smouldering clothes and charred fedora. Ste, unaware of his heroic deed lay curled up, fast asleep on the floor. I carefully walked to the edge of the building to look at the crowd below and there before me lay hundreds of people, all collapsed in heaps fast asleep. I pulled off my mask, desperate for some fresh air. I took in several gulps of clean air and wondered. How am I going to explain this one?

Steam (2017)
by Chris Allton

Embarrassing Dad (2018)
By Chris Allton

The Late Reindeer(2020)
By Chris Allton

Knight School (2021)
By Chris Allton

Please visit
www.chrisallton.co.uk
for more information.

Printed in Great Britain
by Amazon